The Wonderful World of Disney

Walt Disney

ALICE IN WONDERLAND

DERRYDALE BOOKS
New York

Twin Books

It was a hot summer day. Alice and her sister decided to rest under the shade of a big tree. Alice sat on a branch with her cat, Dinah. She made a chain with the daisies she had picked.

Alice's sister leaned against the tree trunk below. She took out a book and started to read aloud. While her sister read, Alice was feeling bored and sleepy. But suddenly she spotted…

...a rabbit running by a pond and across
the field toward them.

Alice saw the White Rabbit take out a large watch from his waistcoat pocket. "Oh, my fur and whiskers! I'm late!" he muttered to himself, looking at his watch with his pink eyes.

"How curious!" Alice thought, and she ran after him. "Where are you going?" she called.

Alice caught up with the Rabbit just in time to see him pop down a large rabbit hole under a hedge. Without a thought, Alice jumped in and started to fall down what seemed to be a deep well.

Alice plunged downward, her skirt puffing up like a parachute. Either the well was very deep, or she was falling very slowly. She had lots of time to look at the various objects that appeared around her—lamps, bookshelves, pictures, mirrors. As she kept falling, Alice didn't even think about how she would get out again. She was too busy wondering what would happen next.

After a long time passed, Alice reached the bottom. She looked up overhead, but everything was dark. In front of her she sighted the Rabbit. He was hurrying along a tunnel. Alice chased after him, for she had many questions to ask him. She turned a corner and ended up in a big windowless hall lit with lamps. There was no sign of the Rabbit.

In the hall, Alice discovered a small, locked door. She peeked through the keyhole and gazed at the loveliest garden she had *ever* seen.

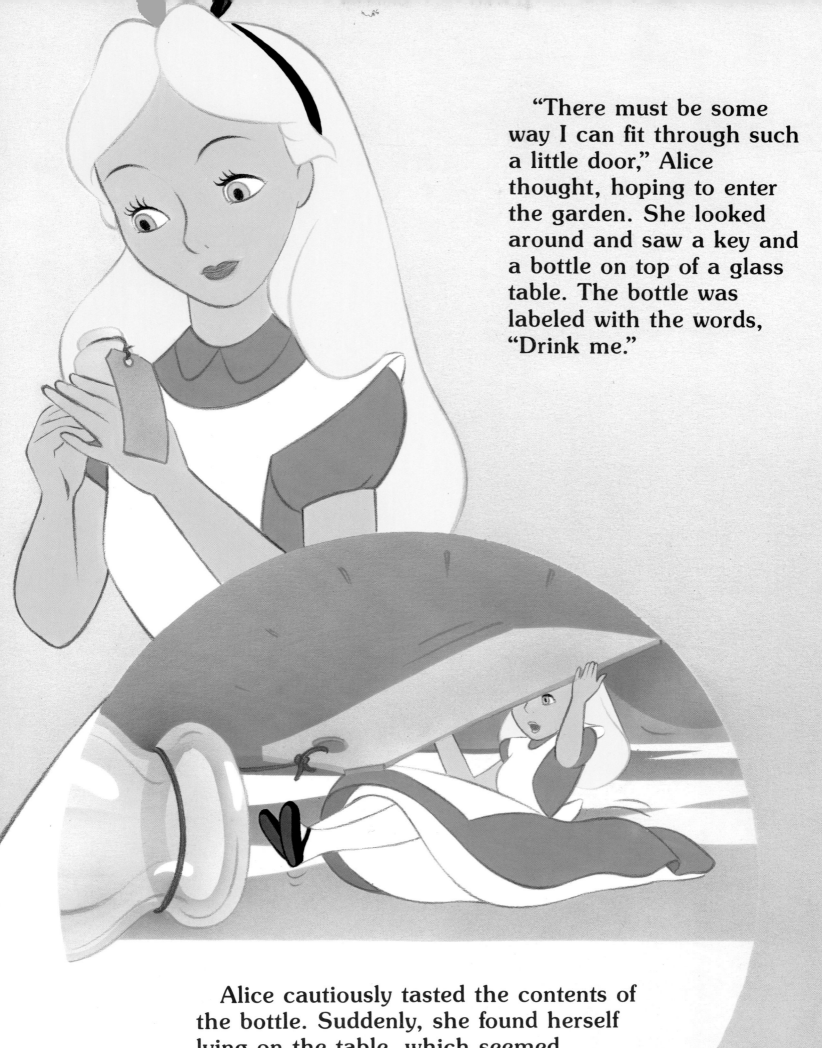

"There must be some way I can fit through such a little door," Alice thought, hoping to enter the garden. She looked around and saw a key and a bottle on top of a glass table. The bottle was labeled with the words, "Drink me."

Alice cautiously tasted the contents of the bottle. Suddenly, she found herself lying on the table, which seemed gigantic. "I'm so small!" she remarked with amazement.

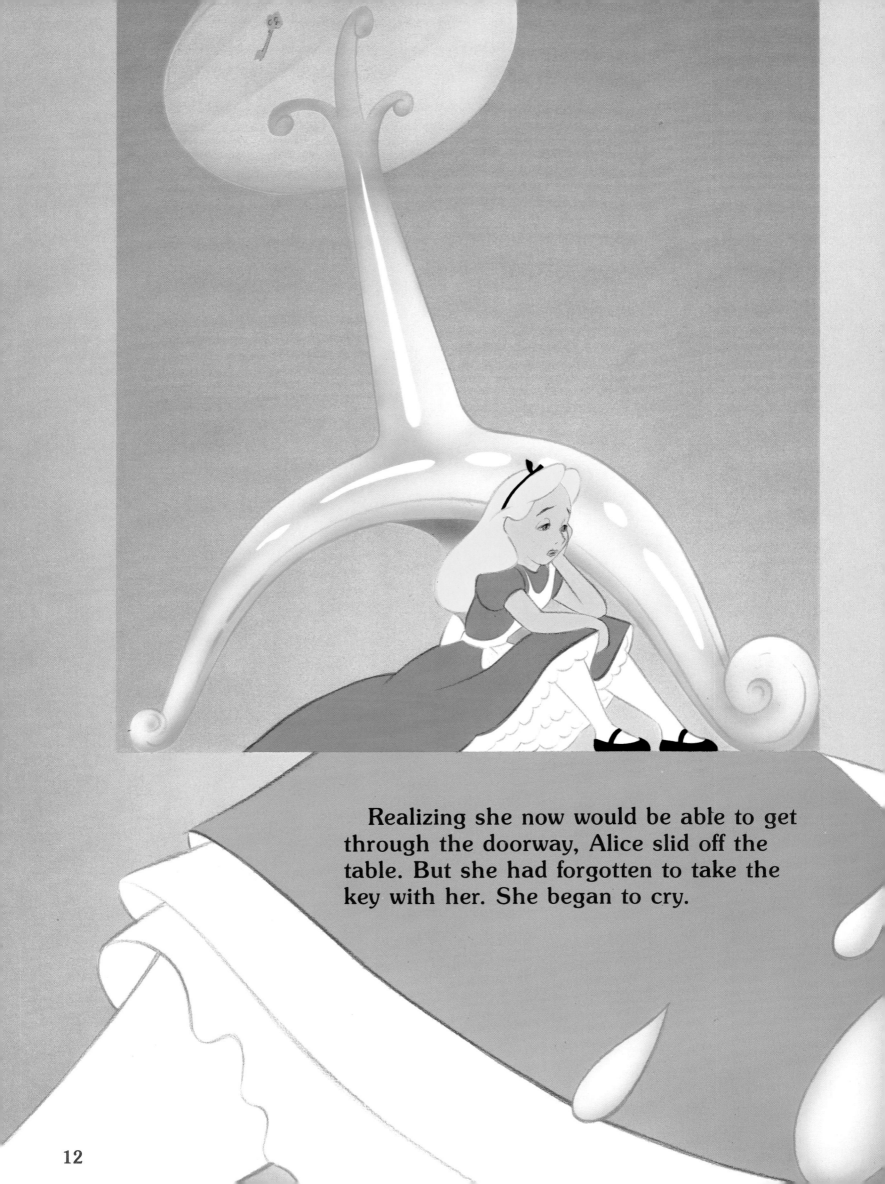

Realizing she now would be able to get through the doorway, Alice slid off the table. But she had forgotten to take the key with her. She began to cry.

"Now I'll never be able to go into the garden," sobbed Alice. But then she noticed a box with the words, "Eat me." The biscuits inside looked delicious, so Alice ate one. At once her hands grew larger. "Good bye, feet!" she said, looking at her feet moving farther away. Feeling like a trapped giant, Alice began crying again, her huge tears streaming down.

Alice then remembered that a few drops remained in the bottle. She drank it, hoping to return to normal size. Instead, she shrank so much that the tears she had shed seemed like a salt-water ocean. "I wish I hadn't cried so much," said Alice as she swam through the keyhole. On the other side of the door, she passed some very strange creatures. When Alice reached land, she saw the Rabbit reach shore and run off. "Wait for me!" she called.

Alice was about to chase after him, when two fat little twins stepped forward. One of them said, "I'm Tweedledee, and he's Tweedledum. Would you like to play hide-and-seek?"

"No, thank you," replied Alice. "I must find the White Rabbit."

"But we've only just met," said one of the twins.

"Sorry. I must go," said Alice, backing
away. She turned and walked down a
path. Soon she came upon a charming
little house. She headed up the walk to
the front door.

Suddenly the White Rabbit appeared, racing up the walk.
When he reached Alice, he blew a trumpet to open the door.
The Rabbit rushed Alice into the house.

"Why, Mary Ann, don't you know what time it is?" the Rabbit scolded her. "Go get my gloves. I'm late!"

Alice was too startled to argue. As she ran up the stairs, she thought, "Goodness! I suppose I'll be taking orders from Dinah next!"

She found the Rabbit's bedroom and started to search. Instead of gloves, she found a cookie jar labeled "Eat me."

Alice was hungry. She ate one cookie and then another. She had hardly finished the second cookie when her head pressed against the ceiling. Her arms pushed out of the windows and her feet stuck out of the doors.

When he saw what had happened, the Rabbit ran upstairs. "Help! Monster!" he yelled when he saw Alice. After the Rabbit calmed down, he had an idea to get rid of the giant and save his house from collapsing. He went out to his garden and picked a carrot. Then he told Alice to eat it.

As soon as Alice nibbled the carrot, she once again began shrinking. She dropped onto the bedroom floor. "Goodness gracious! One can't eat anything around here without changing size like a telescope!" she thought.

Just then the Rabbit remembered his appointment. "Oh, dear! I'm here. I should be there!" he exclaimed, and off he ran.

"Oh, wait!" cried Alice. "Mr. Rabbit! Please! Just a minute!" But the Rabbit was soon out of sight.

On her way down a path, Alice ran into a large bird named Dodo. "Oh, yes. Rabbit went off that way," Dodo said in response to Alice's question.

"Oh, dear! I'll never catch him while I'm this small," sighed Alice.

Alice was still about as big as an ant, and as she approached a field, the grass and flowers seemed like a forest. She ventured into the field and soon realized that she was lost.

Alice bumped into a big mushroom. "Perhaps if I climb on top of this mushroom, I'll be able to spot the Rabbit," she reasoned.

With much difficulty, Alice managed to reach the top of the mushroom. She peered through some blades of grass.

Her eyes met those of a huge caterpillar, who was quietly smoking a pipe.

"Who are you?" he asked, not happy to be interrupted.

"Why, I hardly know, sir," Alice shyly replied. "I've changed so many times this morning, you see."

27

"Explain yourself," said the Caterpillar, puffing smoke at Alice.

"I can't," said Alice. "I'm not myself, you see. Oh, dear! Everything is so confusing!"

"Exactly what is your problem?" asked the Caterpillar.

"I should like to be a little larger, sir," said Alice.

"Then I shall help you," said the Caterpillar. "One side of this mushroom will make you taller, and the other side will make you shorter." Alice immediately pulled off a piece and bit it.

Before Alice had time to wonder what would happen, her head pushed over the top of the trees. On top of her head was a bird's nest.

"I think I overdid it," said Alice, once again a giant. Frightened by the talking tree, the bird flew away.

"How I wish to return to my real size!" said Alice, exhausted by all of the changes. "I'll just eat a bit from the other side of the mushroom," she thought. She took a bite from the piece she was still holding.

Soon she was back to her normal
height. Alice was trying to decide to go...

...when a voice from behind said, "Lose something?" Alice saw a big cat grinning, perched on a tree branch nearby.

Alice asked the cat
which way she ought to go
to find the White Rabbit.
"If you'd really like to
know," the cat replied, "he
went that way."

Alice followed the Cheshire Cat's directions, and she soon
came to a big table set with cups and teapots full of hot tea. At
the table sat the March Hare and the Mad Hatter, singing
about un-birthdays.

The March Hare was serving tea. "You must have a cup of tea," he said to Alice.

Then the Mad Hatter asked, "What day of the month is it?"

Alice answered, "The fourth." The Hatter looked at his watch and sighed, "Two days off! It's worthless!"

Just then Alice saw the White Rabbit run by. As usual, he was looking at his watch. Alice promptly left the tea party to chase the Rabbit.

The Mad Hatter opened his watch and
smeared it with butter. "That'll fix it," he said.
The March Hare started arguing that
the butter would not help. Neither of
them noticed that Alice had left.

Alice was lost once more. She began to cry and wiped her face with a handkerchief in case her tears should cause another flood.

Just then Alice saw the Cheshire Cat sleeping on a branch. She woke him up. "Do something," she said angrily. "You're the one who got me lost!"

"You're not very pleasant," replied the
cat, "but I'll help you anyway." He
pointed her toward a little passageway.

Alice went down the passage, which led into a maze. Alice walked around, feeling trapped until she came to a beautiful garden. It was the one she had seen earlier.

Alice saw three gardeners who looked like playing cards.
They were busily painting the white roses red. "Would you tell
me," Alice asked timidly, "why you are painting these roses?"
"The Queen only likes red roses," they answered.

At that moment, one of the gardeners shouted, "The Queen! The Queen!"

The doors of the palace opened, and a long line of soldiers came out. Like the gardeners, they looked like playing cards. At the end of the procession, the King and Queen of Hearts appeared. The Queen carried a heart-shaped scepter.

The Queen screamed, "Where's the trumpeter? How can the Queen be announced without the trumpet call!"

"Here I am," said the Rabbit, out of breath.

"You're late!" She was about to shout "Off with his head!" when...

...Alice stepped in to distract the Queen. "How do you do, Your Majesty?" she said.

The Queen took a liking to Alice and invited her to play croquet. It was a curious type of croquet game: the balls were live hedgehogs and the mallets were live flamingos. Once Alice got the hang of it, she played quite well. Unfortunately, the Queen hated losing and roared, "Someone's head will roll for this!" Then she pointed at Alice. "Yours!"

At Alice's trial, the Queen pronounced,
"She is guilty! Off with her head!"
Alice protested, "You were the one who
wanted to play, and I won fairly."

49

The Queen's playing-card soldiers started toward Alice.

"I'm not afraid of you," said Alice. "You're just a pack of cards!" Alice started to walk out of the courtroom, but she found herself surrounded by a cloud. She could still hear the Queen's voice, but it sounded faint. Alice whispered sleepily, "Off with her head!"

Suddenly Alice opened her eyes and saw Dinah rubbing against her arm. "Why, I must have been dreaming!" she said. Then she began to tell Dinah and her sister about her adventures.

This 1988 edition published by Derrydale Books, distributed by Crown Publishers, Inc., 225 Park Avenue South New York, New York 10003

Directed by HELENA Productions Ltd.
Image adaptation by Van Gool-Lefevre-Loiseaux

Produced by Twin Books
15 Sherwood Place
Greenwich, CT 06830

Printed and bound in Hong Kong

ISBN 0-517-67008-9

h g f e d c b a

The Wonderful World of Disney